The Greatest Gift

The Greatest Gift

A CHRISTMAS TALE BY
PHILIP VAN DOREN STERN

WITH AN AFTERWORD BY MARGUERITE STERN ROBINSON

GRAPHIC IMAGE
NEW YORK

Foreword

This project began during one of the many Saturdays spent cleaning out my parents' home of 80 years in Floral Park, New York (our mother was born there). Both my parents were involved in publishing their whole lives; my father in design and my mother as a creator of non-fiction indexes which she produced at home on a manual typewriter on books of historical importance. Their collection of books was vast and I was determined to open every one of note in hopes of finding a rare first edition or something saved between the pages and long forgotten. My reward came with the discovery of a small, 32 page book titled *The Greatest Gift*. It was an old and simple book but with illustrations indicating it was made with considerable care. Inside, a dedication to my father read:

> *For Bennett Glazer,*
> *who remembers the movie*
> *With best regards from the author*
> *Philip Van Doren Stern*

Uncertain as to what this meant, I had to research the title and came to the realization that I possessed an original copy of a story that was to become the basis for *It's a Wonderful Life*. Although printed in 1944, Philip presented this to my father after the movie was released. In the Afterword, the author's daughter, Marguerite Robinson, offers a fascinating first-hand account of the origins of what has become perhaps the most beloved American holiday story of all time.

Here, in our second printing, we are reproducing the cover and typography of the original edition in its exact form. The illustrations are untouched and the paging of the text is completely as it appeared in the original – even leaving page 18 blank because in 1944, the letter press printing technique would not prevent the reverse side illustration from showing through.

I hope that you will find, as I did, that reading the text and its history offers you the same feeling of rediscovery of an old friend, but now with a new perspective to enjoy. Even the movie is better after reading and holding the original story of George in your own hands.

Tom Glazer, Publisher, 2012

ORIGINAL ILLUSTRATIONS BY
Rafaello Busoni

THE LITTLE TOWN straggling up the hill was bright with colored Christmas lights. But George Pratt did not see them. He was leaning over the railing of the iron bridge, staring down moodily at the black water. The current eddied and swirled like liquid glass, and occasionally a bit of ice, detached from the shore, would go gliding downstream to be swallowed up in the shadows under the bridge.

The water looked paralyzingly cold. George wondered how long a man could stay alive in it. The glassy blackness had a

5

strange, hypnotic effect on him. He leaned still farther over the railing. . . .

"I wouldn't do that if I were you," a quiet voice beside him said.

George turned resentfully to a little man he had never seen before. He was stout, well past middle age, and his round cheeks were pink in the winter air as though they had just been shaved.

"Wouldn't do what?" George asked sullenly.

"What you were thinking of doing."

"How do you know what I was thinking?"

"Oh, we make it our business to know a lot of things," the stranger said easily.

George wondered what the man's business was. He was a most unremarkable little person, the sort you would pass in a crowd and never notice. Unless you saw his bright blue eyes, that is. You couldn't forget them, for they were the kindest, sharpest eyes you ever saw. Nothing else about him was noteworthy. He wore a moth-eaten old fur cap and a shabby overcoat that was stretched tightly across his paunchy belly. He was carrying a small black satchel. It wasn't a doctor's bag—it was too large for that and not the right shape. It was a salesman's sample kit, George decided distastefully. The fellow was probably some sort of peddler, the kind who would go around poking his sharp little nose into other people's affairs.

"Looks like snow, doesn't it?" the stranger said, glancing up appraisingly at the overcast sky. "It'll be nice to have a white Christmas. They're getting scarce these days—but so are a lot of things." He turned to face George squarely. "You all right now?"

"Of course I'm all right. What made you think I wasn't? I— —"

George fell silent before the stranger's quiet gaze.

The little man shook his head. "You know you shouldn't think of such things—and on Christmas Eve of all times! You've got to consider Mary—and your mother too."

George opened his mouth to ask how this stranger could know his wife's name, but the fellow anticipated him. "Don't ask me how I know such things. It's my business to know 'em. That's why I came along this way tonight. Lucky I did too." He glanced down at the dark water and shuddered.

"Well, if you know so much about me," George said, "give me just one good reason why I should be alive."

The little man made a queer chuckling sound. "Come, come, it can't be that bad. You've got your job at the bank. And Mary and the kids. You're healthy, young, and—"

"And sick of everything!" George cried. "I'm stuck here in this mudhole for life, doing the same dull work day after day. Other men are leading exciting lives, but I—well, I'm just a small-town bank clerk that even the Army didn't want. I never did anything really useful or interesting, and it looks as if I never will. I might just as well be dead. I might better be dead. Sometimes I wish I were. In fact, I wish I'd never been born!"

8

The little man stood looking at him in the growing darkness. "What was that you said?" he asked softly.

"I said I wish I'd never been born," George repeated firmly. "And I mean it too."

The stranger's pink cheeks glowed with excitement. "Why that's wonderful! You've solved everything. I was afraid you were going to give me some trouble. But now you've got the solution yourself. You wish you'd never been born. All right! Okay! You haven't!"

"What do you mean?" George growled.

"You haven't been born. Just that. You haven't been born. No one here knows you. You have no responsibilities—no job —no wife—no children. Why, you haven't even a mother. You couldn't have, of course. All your troubles are over. Your wish, I am happy to say, has been granted—officially."

"Nuts!" George snorted and turned away.

The stranger ran after him and caught him by the arm.

9

"You'd better take this with you," he said, holding out his satchel. "It'll open a lot of doors that might otherwise be slammed in your face."

"What doors in whose face?" George scoffed. "I know everybody in this town. And besides, I'd like to see anybody slam a door in my face."

"Yes, I know," the little man said patiently. "But take this anyway. It can't do any harm and it may help." He opened the satchel and displayed a number of brushes. "You'd be surprised how useful these brushes can be as an introduction—especially the free ones. These, I mean." He hauled out a plain little handbrush. "I'll show you how to use it." He thrust the satchel into George's reluctant hands and began. "When the lady of the house comes to the door you give her this and then talk fast. You say: 'Good evening, madam. I'm from the World Cleaning Company, and I want to present you with this handsome and useful brush absolutely free—no obligation to purchase anything at all.' After that, of course, it's a

10

cinch. Now you try it." He forced the brush into George's hand.

George promptly dropped the brush into the satchel and fumbled with the catch, finally closing it with an angry snap. "Here," he said, and then stopped abruptly, for there was no one in sight.

The little stranger must have slipped away into the bushes growing along the river bank, George thought. He certainly wasn't going to play hide-and-seek with him. It was nearly dark and getting colder every minute. He shivered and turned up his coat collar.

The street lights had been turned on, and Christmas candles in the windows glowed softly. The little town looked remarkably cheerful. After all, the place you grew up in was the one spot on earth where you could really feel at home. George felt a sudden burst of affection even for crotchety old Hank Biddle whose house he was passing. He remembered the quarrel he had had

11

when his car had scraped a piece of bark out of Hank's big maple tree. George looked up at the vast spread of leafless branches towering over him in the darkness. The tree must have been growing there since Indian times. He felt a sudden twinge of guilt for the damage he had done. He had never stopped to inspect the wound, for he was ordinarily afraid to have Hank catch him even looking at the tree. Now he stepped out boldly into the roadway to examine the huge trunk.

Hank must have repaired the scar or painted it over, for there was no sign of it. George struck a match and bent down to look more closely. He straightened up with an odd, sinking feeling in his stomach. There wasn't any scar. The bark was smooth and undamaged.

He remembered what the little man at the bridge had said. It was all nonsense, of course, but the non-existent scar bothered him.

When he reached the bank, he saw that something was wrong. The building was dark, and he knew he had turned the vault light on. He noticed, too, that someone had left the window shades up. He ran around to the front. There was a battered old sign fastened on the door. George could just make out the words:

FOR RENT OR SALE.
Apply JAMES SILVA, *Real Estate.*

Perhaps it was some boys' trick, he thought wildly. Then he saw a pile of ancient leaves and tattered newspapers in the bank's ordinarily immaculate doorway. And the windows looked as though they hadn't been washed in years. A light was still burning across the street in Jim Silva's office. George dashed over and tore the door open.

Jim looked up from his ledgerbook in surprise. "What can I do for you, young man?" he said in the polite voice he reserved for potential customers.

"The bank," George said breathlessly. "What's the matter with it?"

"The old bank building?" Jim Silva turned around and looked out of the window. "Nothing that I can see. Wouldn't like to rent or buy it, would you?"

"You mean—it's out of business?"

"For a good ten years. Went bust during the depression. Stranger 'round these parts, ain't you?"

George sagged against the wall. "I was here some time ago," he said weakly. "The bank was all right then. I even knew some of the people who worked there."

"Didn't know a feller named Marty Jenkins, did you?"

"Marty Jenkins! Why, he—" George was about to say that Marty had never worked at the bank—couldn't have, in fact, for when they had both left school they had applied for a job there and George had gotten it. But now, of course, things were different. He would have to be careful. "No, I didn't know him," he said slowly. "Not really, that is. I'd heard of him."

"Then maybe you heard how he skipped out with fifty thousand dollars. That's why

14

the bank went broke. Pretty near ruined everybody around here." Silva was looking at him sharply. "I was hoping for a minute maybe you'd know where he is. I lost plenty in that crash myself. We'd like to get our hands on Marty Jenkins."

"Didn't he have a brother? Seems to me he had a brother named Arthur."

"Art? Oh, sure. But he's all right. He don't know where his brother went. It's had a terrible effect on him, too. Took to drink, he did. It's too bad—and hard on his wife. He married a nice girl."

George felt the sinking feeling in his stomach again. "Who did he marry?" he demanded hoarsely. Both he and Art had courted Mary.

"Girl named Mary Thatcher," Silva said cheerfully. "She lives up on the hill just this side of the church—Hey! Where are you going?"

But George had bolted out of the office. He ran past the empty bank building and turned up the hill. For a moment he thought of going straight to Mary. The house next to the church had been given them by her father as a wedding present. Naturally Art Jenkins would have gotten it if he had married Mary. George wondered whether they had any children. Then he knew he couldn't face Mary—not yet anyway. He decided to visit his parents and find out more about her.

There were candles burning in the windows of the little weatherbeaten house on the side street, and a Christmas wreath was hanging on the glass panel of the front door. George raised the gate latch with a loud click. A dark shape on the porch jumped up and began to growl. Then it hurled itself down the steps, barking ferociously.

"Brownie!" George shouted. "Brownie, you old fool, stop that! Don't you know me?" But the dog advanced menacingly and drove him back behind the gate. The porch light snapped on, and George's father stepped outside to call the dog off. The barking subsided to a low, angry growl.

His father held the dog by the collar while George cautiously walked past. He could see that his father did not know him. "Is the lady of the house in?" he asked.

His father waved toward the door. "Go on in," he said cordially. "I'll chain this dog up. She can be mean with strangers."

His mother, who was waiting in the hallway, obviously did not recognize him. George opened his sample kit and grabbed the first brush that came to hand. "Good evening, ma'am," he said politely. "I'm from the World Cleaning Company. We're giving out a free sample brush. I thought you might like to have one. No obligation. No obligation at all. . . ." His voice faltered.

His mother smiled at his awkwardness. "I suppose you'll want to sell me something. I'm not really sure I need any brushes."

"No'm, I'm not selling anything," he assured her. "The regular salesman will be around in a few days. This is just—well, just a Christmas present from the company."

"How nice," she said. "You people never gave such good brushes away before."

19

"This is a special offer," he said. His father entered the hall and closed the door.

"Won't you come in for a while and sit down?" his mother said. "You must be tired walking so much."

"Thank you, ma'am. I don't mind if I do." He entered the little parlor and put his bag down on the floor. The room looked different somehow, although he could not figure out why.

"I used to know this town pretty well," he said to make conversation. "Knew some of the townspeople. I remember a girl named Mary Thatcher. She married Art Jenkins, I heard. You must know them."

"Of course," his mother said. "We know Mary well."

"Any children?" he asked casually.

"Two—a boy and a girl."

George sighed audibly. "My, you must be tired," his mother said. "Perhaps I can get you a cup of tea."

"No'm, don't bother," he said. "I'll be having supper soon." He looked around the little parlor, trying to find out why it looked different. Over the mantelpiece hung a framed photograph which had been taken on his kid brother Harry's sixteenth birthday. He remembered how they had gone to Potter's studio to be photographed together. There was something queer about the picture. It took him a full minute to realize what it was. It showed only one figure—Harry's.

"That your son?" he asked.

His mother's face clouded. She nodded but said nothing.

"I think I met him, too," George said hesitantly. "His name's Harry, isn't it?"

His mother turned away, making a strange choking noise in her throat. Her husband put his arm clumsily around her shoulder. His voice, which was always mild and gentle, suddenly became harsh. "You couldn't have met him," he said. "He's been dead a long while. He was drowned the day that picture was taken."

George's mind flew back to the long-ago August afternoon when he and Harry had visited Potter's studio. On their way home

21

they had gone swimming. Harry had been seized with a cramp, he remembered. He had pulled him out of the water and had thought nothing of it. But suppose he hadn't been there!

"I'm sorry," he said miserably. "I guess I'd better go. I hope you like the brush. And I wish you both a very Merry Christmas." There, he had put his foot in it again, wishing them a Merry Christmas when they were thinking about their dead son.

Brownie tugged fiercely at her chain as George went down the porch steps and accompanied his departure with a hostile, rolling growl.

He wanted desperately now to see Mary. He wasn't sure he could stand not being recognized by her, but he had to see her.

The lights were on in the church, and the choir was making last-minute preparations for Christmas vespers. The organ had been practicing "Holy Night" evening after evening until George had become thoroughly sick of it. But now the music almost tore his heart out.

He stumbled blindly up the path to his own house. The lawn was untidy, and the flower bushes he had kept carefully trimmed were neglected and badly sprouted. Art Jenkins could hardly be expected to care for such things.

When he knocked at the door there was a long silence, followed by the shout of a child. Then Mary came to the door.

At the sight of her, George's voice almost failed him. "Merry Christmas, ma'am," he managed to say at last. His hand shook as he tried to open the satchel.

"Come in," Mary said indifferently. "It's cold out."

When George entered the living room, unhappy as he was, he could not help noticing with a secret grin that the too-high-priced blue sofa they often had quarreled over was there. Evidently Mary had gone through the same thing with Art Jenkins and had won the argument with him too.

George got his satchel open. One of the brushes had a bright blue handle and vari-colored bristles. It was obviously a brush not intended to be given away, but George didn't care. He handed it to Mary. "This would be fine for your sofa," he said.

"My, that's a pretty brush," she exclaimed. "You're giving it away free?"

He nodded solemnly. "Special introductory offer. It's one way for the company to keep excess profits down—share them with its friends."

She stroked the sofa gently with the brush, smoothing out the velvety nap. "It is a nice brush. Thank you. I—" There was a sudden scream from the kitchen, and two small children rushed in. A little, homely-faced girl flung herself into her mother's arms, sobbing loudly as a boy of seven came running after her, snapping a toy pistol at her head. "Mommy, she won't die," he yelled. "I shot her a hunert times, but she won't die."

He looks just like Art Jenkins, George thought. Acts like him too. The boy sud-

24

denly turned his attention to him. "Who're you?" he demanded belligerently. He pointed his pistol at George and pulled the trigger. "You're dead!" he cried. "You're dead. Why don't you fall down and die?"

There was a heavy step on the porch. The boy looked frightened and backed away. George saw Mary glance apprehensively at the door.

Art Jenkins came in. He stood for a moment in the doorway, clinging to the knob for support. His eyes were glazed, and his face was very red. "Who's this?" he demanded thickly.

"He's a brush salesman," Mary tried to explain. "He gave me this brush."

"Brush salesman!" Art sneered. "Well, tell him to get outa here. We don't want no brushes," Art hiccoughed violently and lurched across the room to the sofa where he sat down suddenly. "An' we don't want no brush salesmen neither."

"You'd better go," Mary whispered to George. "I'm sorry."

The boy edged toward George. "G'wan,

25

go 'way. We don't want no brushes. An' we don't want no ole brush salesmen neither."

George looked despairingly at Mary. Her eyes were begging him to go. Art had lifted his feet up on the sofa and was sprawling out on it, muttering unkind things about brush salesmen. George went to the door, followed by Art's son who kept snapping his pistol at him and saying: "You're dead—dead—dead!"

Perhaps the boy was right, George thought when he reached the porch. Maybe he was dead, or maybe this was all a bad dream from which he might eventually awake. He wanted to find the little man on the bridge again and try to persuade him to cancel the whole deal.

He hurried down the hill and broke into a run when he neared the river. George was relieved to see the little stranger standing on the bridge. "I've had enough," he gasped. "Get me out of this—you got me into it."

The stranger raised his eyebrows. "I got you into it! I like that! You were granted your wish. You got everything you asked

26

for. You're the freest man on earth now. You have no ties. You can go anywhere—do anything. What more can you possibly want?"

"Change me back," George pleaded. "Change me back—please. Not just for my sake but for others too. You don't know what a mess this town is in. You don't understand. I've got to get back. They need me here."

"I understand right enough," the stranger said slowly. "I just wanted to make sure you did. You had the greatest gift of all conferred upon you—the gift of life, of being a part of this world and taking a part in it. Yet you denied that gift." As the stranger spoke, the church bell high up on the hill sounded, calling the townspeople to Christmas vespers. Then the downtown church bell started ringing.

"I've got to get back," George said desperately. "You can't cut me off like this. Why, it's murder!"

"Suicide rather, wouldn't you say?" the stranger murmured. "You brought it on

27

yourself. However, since it's Christmas Eve —well, anyway, close your eyes and keep listening to the bells." His voice sank lower. "Keep listening to the bells. . . ."

George did as he was told. He felt a cold, wet snowdrop touch his cheek—and then another and another. When he opened his eyes, the snow was falling fast, so fast that it obscured everything around him. The little stranger could not be seen, but then neither could anything else. The snow was so thick that George had to grope for the bridge railing.

As he started toward the village, he thought he heard someone saying: "Merry Christmas," but the bells were drowning out all rival sounds, so he could not be sure.

When he reached Hank Biddle's house he stopped and walked out into the roadway, peering down anxiously at the base of the big maple tree. The scar was there, thank Heaven! He touched the tree affectionately. He'd have to do something about the wound —get a tree surgeon or something. Anyway, he'd evidently been changed back. He was himself again. Maybe it was all a dream, or perhaps he had been hypnotized by the smooth-flowing black water. He had heard of such things.

At the corner of Main and Bridge Streets he almost collided with a hurrying figure. It was Jim Silva, the real estate agent. "Hello, George," Jim said cheerfully. "Late tonight, ain't you? I should think you'd want to be home early on Christmas Eve."

George drew a long breath. "I just wanted to see if the bank is all right. I've got to make sure the vault light is on."

"Sure it's on. I saw it as I went past."

"Let's look, huh?" George said, pulling at Silva's sleeve. He wanted the assurance of a witness. He dragged the surprised real estate dealer around to the front of the bank where the light was gleaming through the falling snow. "I told you it was on," Silva said with some irritation.

"I had to make sure," George mumbled. "Thanks—and Merry Christmas!" Then he was off like a streak, running up the hill.

He was in a hurry to get home, but not in

such a hurry that he couldn't stop for a moment at his parents' house, where he wrestled with Brownie until the friendly old bulldog waggled all over with delight. He grasped his startled brother's hand and wrung it frantically, wishing him an almost hysterical Merry Christmas. Then he dashed across the parlor to examine a certain photograph. He kissed his mother, joked with his father, and was out of the house a few seconds later, stumbling and slipping on the newly fallen snow as he ran on up the hill.

The church was bright with light, and the choir and the organ were going full tilt. George flung the door to his home open and called out at the top of his voice: "Mary! Where are you? Mary! Kids!"

His wife came toward him, dressed for going to church, and making gestures to silence him. "I've just put the children to bed," she protested. "Now they'll—" But not another word could she get out of her mouth, for he smothered it with kisses, and then he dragged her up to the children's room, where he violated every tenet of parental behavior

by madly embracing his son and his daughter and waking them up thoroughly.

It was not until Mary got him downstairs that he began to be coherent. "I thought I'd lost you. Oh, Mary, I thought I'd lost you!"

"What's the matter, darling?" she asked in bewilderment.

He pulled her down on the sofa and kissed her again. And then, just as he was about to tell her about his queer dream, his fingers came in contact with something lying on the seat of the sofa. His voice froze.

He did not even have to pick the thing up, for he knew what it was. And he knew that it would have a blue handle and vari-colored bristles.

Afterword
Marguerite Stern Robinson

My father, Philip Van Doren Stern, was shaving on Saturday morning, February 12, 1938, while he explored the idea for the story *The Greatest Gift*—which became the basis for the movie, *It's a Wonderful Life*. The idea had come from a dream he had during the night. As he wrote in his notes: "The idea came to me complete from start to finish—a most unusual occurrence, as any writer will tell you, for ordinarily a story has to be struggled with, changed around and mixed up." In contrast to his other writings, mainly on history, he said that the idea for *The Greatest Gift* had emerged full blown, and he had never considered changing it. What he had to do, he said, was to learn to write it.

In April 1938, my father wrote the first draft of *The Greatest Gift*. "I was just learning to write fiction, so that first version was pretty terrible. Fortunately, I knew it was, so I had the sense to put it away. A few years later I tried again. The results were still no good." He waited until the spring of 1943 before rewriting the story and showing it to his agent, who said that she liked it but that it would be difficult to sell a fantasy to the magazines. My father wrote, "After she had tried everything from *The Saturday Evening*

Post to farm journals, it was evident that no magazine would touch it. By this time, I had become fond of the story that nobody wanted. I revised it again and had 200 twenty-four-page pamphlets printed at my own expense. I sent these out as Christmas cards for Christmas, 1943."

I was in the third grade then and remember delivering a few of these cards to my teachers and to my friends, who were children from families of a variety of backgrounds and religions. My father, who was himself from a mixed religious background, explained to me that while this story takes place at Christmas time and that we were sending it as a Christmas card to our friends, it is a universal story for all people in all times.

A few months later, in March 1944, I answered the telephone one evening in our home in Brooklyn. It was a Western Union operator who asked to speak to my father—and I knew that in 1944 receiving a telegram often meant bad news. My father took the phone, listened to the operator read the telegram, and then turned to my mother saying, "Hold me up! I can't believe it." I thought something terrible had happened. It was, however, a telegram from my father's agent, announcing that she had received an offer from a well-known studio for the movie rights to *The Greatest Gift*. My father agreed, and planning began in Hollywood.

During World War II, my father was an editor and member of the Planning Board for Armed Services Editions (1941-43), and General Manager of Editions for the Armed Services (1943-45). Many kinds of books were selected and produced on a large scale—in volumes sized to fit into the pockets of armed services uniforms. People who returned home after the war often told him how much those books meant to them, and how they had helped to keep up morale. After the war, he worked in publishing and advertising, but he was a writer at heart. When an interviewer asked him about his interests, he said, "I'm interested in knowledge." He wrote or edited more than forty books on a wide range of topics, with many on different aspects of the Civil War.

Shortly after the war ended, Frank Capra was discharged from the Army, and returned to the United States. After reading *The Greatest Gift*, he became excited about its possibilities as a film, and wanted Jimmy Stewart for the leading role. A highly decorated World War II hero, Stewart heard about the story in the fall of 1945, just after he had been discharged from the Air Force. "I got a telephone call [from] Frank Capra... He said, 'I've got an idea for a story... Come on over to the house and I'll tell you.' So I went over... The two main ideas were: one, no one is born to be a failure; and two, no one is poor who has friends... He told me all this, but then he said, 'I don't know... I don't know.' I said, "Frank, PLEASE! I think it's wonderful!' "[1]

In an interview for *American Film* published in October 1978, Capra said: "[This] was my first picture after having been in uniform and out of theatrical films for five years. I was scared to death... We were at RKO and Charles Koerner, the studio head, came in. [He said] 'I've got just the story for you. You've got to read it. We've got three scripts on it'... I said, 'Well, what about the scripts?' He said, 'Oh, they missed the idea.' 'What idea?' 'The idea I paid for when I bought this Christmas card. I paid $50,000 for it...' 'You paid $50,000 for a Christmas card? Boy, I've got to see *that* 'Christmas card.' And there it was...a story about a man who thought he was a failure and who was given the opportunity to come back and see the world as it would have been had he not been born. Well, my goodness, this thing hit me like a ton of bricks."

Capra wrote about *The Greatest Gift*: "It was the story

I had been looking for all my life! Small town. A man, a good man, ambitious. But so busy helping others, life seems to pass him by. He wishes he'd never been born. He gets his wish. Through the eyes of a guardian angel he sees the world as it would have been had he never been born. Wow! What an idea. The kind of an idea that when I get old and sick and scared and ready to die—they'd still say 'He made *The Greatest Gift*.' "[7]

The screenplay by Frances Goodrich and Albert Hackett was widely acclaimed, and *It's a Wonderful Life*, the film based on *The Greatest Gift*, was released in December 1946. *Life* magazine ran two articles on it, and it was broadcast from coast to coast by CBS, and in other parts of the world by the State Department. The world premiere was held on December 20, 1946 at the Globe Theater in New York, for the benefit of the Boys' Club of New York. We were relieved to discover, at the premiere and after the movie was released, that we were not alone in our enthusiasm for *It's a Wonderful Life*. Many people loved the movie and said they watched it over and over. While not originally a box office success, over time *It's a Wonderful Life* became immensely popular—eventually, a Christmas classic.

Jimmy Stewart wrote to my father on December 31,

1946, "More important than anything, thank you for giving us that idea, which I think is the best one that anyone has had for a long time. It was an inspiration for everyone concerned with the picture to work in it, because everyone seemed to feel that the fundamental story was so sound and right, and that story was yours, and you should be justly proud of it."

Starting with those 200 Christmas cards, the messages of my father's story have reached millions of people. Many who have read *The Greatest Gift* have told me over the years that they love the story and read it often. And many more who have seen the film have said that *It's a Wonderful Life* is their favorite of all movies. It doesn't seem to matter who they are, or what they do. Age, gender, occupation, race, religion, income level, nationality, politics—none of these factors seems to make any difference when it comes to the people who say this is their favorite film. In 2007, the American Film Institute ranked *It's a Wonderful Life* as number twenty of the 100 greatest movies of all time; in 2008, it was also ranked third on AFI's top ten fantasy films of all time.

After the film's premiere, my father sent one of the original Christmas cards to Frank Capra, who replied: "I thank you for sending it and I love you for creating it." Capra referred to my father as the man whose Christmas tale "was the spark that set me off into making my favorite film, *It's a Wonderful Life.*" Much later, Jimmy Stewart said that of the more than seventy films he had made, this was his favorite.[3]

In his autobiography, Capra wrote of *It's a Wonderful Life,* "I thought it was the greatest film I ever made. Better yet, I thought it was the greatest film anybody had ever made."[4]

He described the theme in this way: "*It's a Wonderful Life* sums up my philosophy of film making. First, to exalt the *worth* of the individual. Second, to champion *man*—plead his causes, protest any degradation of his dignity, spirit, or divinity. And third, to dramatize the viability of the individual—as in the theme of the film itself... There is a radiance and glory in the darkness, could we but see, and to see we have only to look. I beseech you to look."[5]

Nearly seventy years after *The Greatest Gift* was written and *It's a Wonderful Life* opened at the Boys' Club of New York, the themes of story and film, and the views, convictions, and passions of the characters, seem to be still considered relevant to our lives today. Why do George Bailey, Henry Potter, and others appear in the press and other media so many decades later—as we today struggle with a variety of economic, financial, and moral issues and controversies? Three quite different examples indicate the breadth of story and film, and suggest their relevance in the twenty-first century.

Financial inclusion

George Bailey (Jimmy Stewart) runs the Bailey Brothers Building & Loan Association, a firm providing commercial financial services to many in and around the (fictional) town of Bedford Falls. Many of the Building & Loan's clients are among the town's low income population, who made good use of their mortgage loans and other financial products—and over time were able to build a small house, increase their income, and improve their lives. But Henry Potter (Lionel Barrymore), majority shareholder in Bailey Building & Loan, and George's nemesis, aims to stop the Building & Loan from providing home loans and other financial services to the working poor. Wealthy, powerful, corrupt, and ruthless, Potter plans to gain control of the firm (his interest in real estate is in renting rundown slum shacks to poor people at high rents). Having already taken control of the bank, the bus line, and the department stores in Bedford Falls, Potter now prepares to take over the Bailey Building & Loan Association.

George and Mr. Potter would be quite at home in today's controversies about mortgages, bank failures and home foreclosures. The headline of a November 2008 article on the recession in *The New York Times* asks: "What Would George Bailey Do?" The author, Edward Rothstein, looks at *It's a Wonderful Life* for possible parallels or analogies that might help in understanding the current recession. "[George] stopped a run on the Bailey Brothers Building & Loan Association that would have destroyed it...[But] his predicament, with its eerie prefiguration of the present, provokes a closer look at the crossroads in which culture and finance intersect."[6]

As the 2008 recession developed, and its depth and potential duration became increasingly apparent, Mr. Potter and his financial manipulations, profit strategies, and outright theft—have been frequently remembered and compared with their large-scale modern equivalents. George Bailey, too, has been widely quoted and cited. In a letter to *The New York Times* published on Christmas Day 2008, Tom King of West St. Paul, Minnesota, wrote: "What's gotten us in this huge pickle today is the take-the-money schemes of the Mr. Potters of the world. What can save us are the honesty and concern for others of the

Georges of the world. George's angel, Clarence, needs to get busy now that he's earned his wings."[7]

The awesome power of apparent insignificance in history. With the Potter-engineered problems for the Bailey Building & Loan, George becomes deeply depressed and decides to commit suicide. His guardian angel, Clarence, is sent from Heaven to help him, and he saves George's life. George tells Clarence he wishes he had never been born. Clarence grants his wish, and George learns what the world would have been like without him. No one in Bedford Falls recognizes him, and even his parents have no use for this stranger. As a child, George had saved his brother Harry from drowning; during the war Harry saved the lives of all on his troop ship. But in the alternative reality that Clarence had set up for George, all of them had died. And George begins to understand also what happened when the Building & Loan collapsed, and when Bedford Falls became Pottersville.

The distinguished natural historian Stephen Jay Gould refers to *It's a Wonderful Life* in the introduction to his book *Wonderful Life: The Burgess Shale and the Nature of History,* which is about the evolution of organisms. "The title of the book expresses the duality of our wonder—at the beauty of the organisms themselves, and at the new view of life that they have inspired....This theme is central to the most memorable scene in America's most beloved film—Jimmy Stewart's guardian angel replaying life's tape without him and demonstrating the awesome power of apparent insignificance in history."[8] Gould wrote me, saying: "Now that I read your father's book, I realize that the key scene...that served as my inspiration... is in fact the source of the entire idea for the movie... I was delighted to recognize how faithful and respectful Capra was to its meaning and intent."

George begs to be returned to his life—and Clarence grants his wish. George is then home in Bedford Falls—and with widespread support from his family and his many friends, neighbors, and clients, he can now continue and expand the Bailey Building & Loan—providing decent, affordable, housing and other financial services. And George has learned that he and his work are indeed significant. Mr. Potter will still be there, but there will be choices, and lessons for others.

Human Life and the Inner Mind

In a 2011 article called "Social Animal," David Brooks examines "a debate in our culture about what really makes us happy, which is summarized by, on the one hand, the book *On the Road* [by Jack Kerouac] and, on the other, the movie *It's a Wonderful Life*. The former celebrates the life of freedom and adventure. The latter celebrates roots and connections. Research over the past thirty years makes it clear that what the inner mind really wants is connection. *It's a Wonderful Life* was right."[9]

My father would be very happy to know that *The Greatest Gift* and *It's a Wonderful Life* live on—and not only in the past. People today still think of, cite, write, argue, and perhaps learn from, those living in the fictional Bedford Falls so many decades ago. The film and the story on which it is based have reached and influenced millions of people. I am one of them. For over three decades I have worked extensively on the development of commercial microfinance in Asia, Africa, and Latin America, primarily as an advisor to large banks and others providing financial services to many millions of economically active poor people, previously excluded from formal financial services. And I have long experience as a policy advisor to finance ministries, central banks, and commercial banks. But it was not until 2001 when I was writing the preface to the first volume of my book, *The Microfinance Revolution,* that I realized fully how much of my lifetime career is owed to the underlying influences of *The Greatest Gift* and *It's a Wonderful Life.* George Bailey, Mr. Potter, Mary, Clarence, Frank Capra, and of course my father, have had a major effect on my life in microbanking—which continues still.

I was the only child of my parents, Philip Van Doren Stern and Lillian Diamond Stern, Our family—my late husband, Allan Richard Robinson, and our three daughters, Sarah Penelopeque Robinson, Perrine Robinson-Geller, and Laura Ondine Robinson; our wonderful sons-in-law, grandchildren and other family members, are heirs to more than my father's literary property, we are the heirs to his ideas and his values. We hope that this book will bring joy to those who already know and love the film classic, and that it will reach a broad audience of all generations. *The Greatest Gift* is as compelling today as it was nearly 70 years ago because, in this story, lies a powerful message about the significance of the lives of all of us. As for its author, Philip Van Doren

Stern, I borrow a line from George Bailey's brother, Harry: "He was the richest man in town."

Notes

1 Jeanine Basinger, Frances Goodrich, Leonard Maltin and the Trustees of the Frank Capra Archives, *The "It's a Wonderful Life" Book* (New York: Alfred A. Knopf, 1986), p. 77.

2 Frank Capra, *The Name Above the Title: An Autobiography* (New York: Macmillan, 1971; Bantam, 1972), p. 417.

3 Basinger et al., *The "It's a Wonderful Life" Book*, p. 85.

4 Capra, *The Name Above the Title: An Autobiography.*

5 Basinger et al., *The "It's a Wonderful Life" Book*, p. ix.

6 Associated Press, *The New York Times*, p. C–1, November 4, 2008.

7 Associated Press, *The New York Times*, Letters, p. A–22, December 25, 2008.

8 Stephen Jay Gould, *Wonderful Life: The Burgess Shale and the Nature of History,* (New York: W.W. Norton, 1989), p, 14.

9 Condé Nast, *The New Yorker,* p. 28, January 17, 2011.

Published by Graphic Image
305 Spagnoli Road,
Melville, NY 11747, USA
www.graphicimage.com

First published 1944
Copyright © Philip Van Doren Stern, 1943
Copyright © renewed Philip Van Doren
Stern, 1971

Revised edition first published 2011
Second vintage edition published 2012
Copyright © Philip Van Doren Stern, 1943
Afterword Copyright © The Greatest Gift
Corporation, 2011

Original Illustrations: Rafaello Busoni

All Distribution
Graphic Image, 305 Spagnoli Road,
Melville, NY 11747, USA
To order (USA) call +1 800 232 5550
or e-mail customerservice@graphicimage.com
www.graphicimage.com

Library of Congress Cataloguing-in-
Publication Data

Trade Edition
ISBN: 978-0-9839476-0-8 (Graphic Image)
ISBN: 978-0-9570255-0-9

Leather Edition
ISBN: 978-0-615-52456-6 (Graphic Image)
ISBN: 978-0-9570255-1-6

Copyright, 1943, 1944 By
Philip Van Doren Stern

This book was printed on 100 lb Superfine
Eggshell text paper and typeset in Berkeley
Oldstyle Book.

GRAPHIC IMAGE